The Three Wishes

The Three Wishes

A Collection of Puerto Rican Folktales

Selected and adapted by
RICARDO E. ALEGRÍA

Translated by Elizabeth Culbert
Illustrated by Lorenzo Homar

Harcourt, Brace & World, Inc., New York

Foreword

The island of Puerto Rico was one of the first Caribbean islands to be settled by the Spanish Conquistadores, who soon subdued the native Taino Indians and began to import Negro slaves from the west coast of Africa to work in the sugar plantations. Thus the three great races of humanity—the Mongolian represented by the Tainos, the Caucasian represented by the Spaniards, and the Negro represented by the Africans—were mingled. As a result, the Puerto Rican culture, though basically Hispanic, reflects elements of the aboriginal and of the African cultures.

These elements are to be found in the folktales that have been handed from father to son over four centuries. Some of these traditional stories originated in the Orient and were carried to Spain by the Arabs when they invaded and lived there for eight centuries. Others were brought from West Africa by the Negro slaves. After countless retellings they have been adapted to the geography and cultural environment of Puerto Rico.

As presented here, the folktales have been slightly adapted for children, but the themes and details of the traditional versions have been preserved. We hope they will serve as a pleasant introduction to the rich folklore of Puerto Rico.

Contents

The Animal Musicians

(LOS ANIMALES MUSICOS)

There was once a farmer who had a donkey (burro) so old that he could no longer pull a cart. The farmer told his wife that he had decided to kill the useless donkey. The donkey heard this, and that very night when everyone was asleep, he escaped into the woods. He ran as fast as he could to get as far away as possible from his master's house.

After a while he met a goat who was pulling at a rope that tethered him. The donkey asked what was the matter, and the goat said he was trying to get away because his master was going to kill him now that he was old and useless. The donkey said he would help; with his teeth, he cut the rope and freed the goat. Together, they set out to see the world.

As they were walking through a distant country, they met a dog. His tongue was hanging out—he was so exhausted from running. The donkey and the goat stopped him and asked what was the matter, and the dog, panting, said that he had run for two days and two nights trying to escape, because now that he was old and could no longer guard the sheep, his master had decided to kill him. The donkey and the goat told him their stories; then they all talked together for a while about the ungratefulness of men who kill animals when they become old and useless. The donkey and the goat invited the dog to join them in their travels around the world. The dog accepted as he was lonesome.

That night they slept beneath a tree, and at midnight they were awakened by a mewing sound. They searched and found a cat who was almost dead from hunger. They fed him, and after he had eaten, he told them that his master had turned him out of the house because he was old and could no longer catch mice. The animals told him to stop worrying and to come along with them to see the world. So the donkey, the goat, the dog, and the cat went on together, keeping well away from men, whom they considered to be ungrateful beings.

One day as they were crossing a border into another country, a rooster came running by. The animals asked him what was the matter and where was he going. He answered that he was running away from his master, who wanted to kill him now that he was old and scrawny and no longer the Cock of the Roost. The animals told him to cheer up, that men had been as unjust to them, too, and that they had formed a society and were going to live together and enjoy traveling around the world. The rooster asked if he might join them, and they said yes and continued on their way.

For a long time they journeyed together, always taking care to avoid men. But after a while they began to tire of idle traveling and wondered what they could do to earn a living and to become useful to men again. It was then that the rooster suggested forming an orchestra and making music and singing. The rooster was proud of his voice, and the cat, also, admitted that *he* could sing. After discussing it a while, they decided that the rooster, the cat, and the dog would be singers and the donkey and the goat would drum on wood with their feet to beat time and mark the rhythm.

Very pleased with their plan for remaking their lives and becoming useful again so that they would no longer have to travel from place to place, hiding in the woods, they decided to give a serenade at the first house they came to to demonstrate to men that they were useful and worthy of living. They told the rooster to fly up into a tree and look over the neighborhood to see if there was a house nearby.

The rooster flew to the top of the highest tree and looked about. He saw a light in the distance and called to his friends that he had spotted a house. The other animals told him to hurry down, that they were going to give their first serenade at that house. In a short time they reached the house. They knew there were people inside as they could see a light and hear noises. The animals crept quietly up to the window to surprise the inhabitants with their music. The window was very

high, so they formed a ladder—the goat climbed on
the donkey's back, the dog climbed on the goat's back,
the cat climbed on the dog, and the rooster perched
on the cat's back. When all had taken their positions,
they began the concert. They sang and drummed on
the wooden planks of the house. The donkey kicked
the wall with his feet while the goat butted it with
his head and horns. The dog barked with all his might,
and the cat yowled while the rooster crowed. Now
it so happened that the men in the house were a
band of robbers. The noise the animals made was so
loud and terrifying that the robbers thought a platoon
of soldiers had come for them. They ran away as fast
as they could go, never stopping to see what the noise
was all about.

The animals, seeing their audience run away, were
very sad and upset. This was not what they had planned!
They were tired and hungry, too, so they went into
the house to spend the night and to look for something
to eat. They ate the food the robbers had left and then
lay down to sleep. The rooster perched above the door,
the cat curled up on the kitchen hearth, the dog lay
down by the door, the goat stayed in the dining room,
and the donkey slept in the bedroom.

After running away and hiding for a while, the robbers sent the bravest one back as a spy to see if the
soldiers had left. When he reached the house and heard
no noise, he thought it was empty, so he went in. It

was very dark, and he went to the kitchen to get a
light. He saw two glowing spots on the floor, which
he thought were live coals, and stooped down to get
them. A sharp knife cut his hand! The bandit cried
out in pain and ran from the kitchen without discov-
ering that the glowing coals were the cat's eyes shining
in the dark and that the cuts on his hand were cat
scratches. He ran into the bedroom and tripped over
the donkey who kicked him into the dining room, where
the goat butted him to the door, where the dog bit him
on the leg and the rooster dropped from the lintel overhead and clawed at his back and arms.

The robber was bleeding and terrified by the time he
got back to his companions. He told them to run—
that the house was filled with strong armed men who
had almost killed him. When he had gone into the
kitchen, one of them stabbed him seven times, another
strong one had knocked him down, another had struck
him on the shoulders with his sword, another had given
him a blow on the leg with his hatchet, while another,
jabbing him with a knife, had shouted: "Kick-him-to-
mee! Kick-him-to-meee!"

The robbers, hearing this and seeing the condition of
their companion, lost no time in getting away.

As for the animals, they stayed on in the house, and
every night they made their music. People, hearing it,
thought the Devil had taken possession, so, needless to
say, they never went near the house and the animals
were left to live happily, undisturbed by men.

The Three Brothers and the Marvelous Things

(LOS TRES HERMANOS Y LAS COSAS MARAVILLOSAS)

Once upon a time, in a distant country, there was a king who had an only daughter, and she was very beautiful. Three princes, who were brothers, were in love with her, and each one wanted her for his wife. Neither the King nor the Princess knew which one to choose as all were good men, handsome, brave, and true.

Not knowing what else to do, the King called the three brothers to the castle and explained that, because he had only one daughter and did not know which one of them to choose as his son-in-law, he had decided to test them. Each was to go out into the world and at the end of a year to return, bringing, as a gift to the King, the most marvelous thing he had found during his travels. The one who brought the most marvelous thing in the world was to marry the Princess. The other two would be awarded other kingdoms to rule.

This sounded fair enough to the three young men, so they accepted the King's conditions. That very day, after receiving the King's blessing and a handkerchief each from the Princess, they mounted their horses and rode off in search of the most marvelous thing in the world.

After many days they came to a place where the road branched out in three directions. Here the brothers parted, saying good-by to each other and agreeing to meet in the same place at the end of ten months to return home together. Each one set out by a different road. The eldest brother took the road to the left, and after having crossed many countries and undergone many adventures without finding anything marvelous enough to bring to the King, he came upon an old woman as he was crossing a desert. She asked him for water. The youth had very little water left, but as he was kind and sympathetic, he gave what he had to the old woman. She was a witch, and she asked him what he was doing out there in the desert; so he told her his story. Then the old woman told him that, since he had been so generous, she would help him to find the most marvelous thing in that region, which was a magic carpet. A little farther along, she explained, there lived a dwarf who was the owner of the carpet. He never slept; he stayed awake all day and all night, guarding his carpet. Then the old woman took some magic powder out of a bag and gave it to the young man, telling him to throw it into the dwarf's well when the dwarf wasn't looking. The youth was very happy at the thought of obtaining the magic carpet, and after thanking the old woman for her help, he galloped off in search of the dwarf's house.

Before he reached it, he made a large figure of straw and dressed it in his own cloak and cap. Then he mounted it on his horse, and as he neared the dwarf's house, he whipped the horse and sent it flying by while he himself hid behind a tree.

When the dwarf heard the horse, he rushed out with his dogs, thinking that someone had come to steal his magic carpet. He sped after the horse and its rider. The youth took advantage of his absence to throw the powder into the dwarf's well; then he climbed a tree to wait for him to return with the dogs.

When they did return, both the dwarf and his dogs were exhausted by the chase. They went straight to the well for a drink of water, and as soon as it touched their lips, they fell to the ground in a profound sleep. Then the youth climbed down from the tree and went into the dwarf's house to search for the magic carpet. He found it in a box under the bed and took it to the yard. There he spread it out, sat down upon it, and bade it carry him to the fork in the road where he was to meet his brothers. At once the magic carpet rose through the air, and in a few minutes he reached the meeting place. Since he was a few days early and the first to arrive, he built a little straw house and waited there for his brothers.

Meantime, the second brother, who had taken the middle road, had traveled through many countries of dark-skinned people. Although he had had many in-

teresting adventures and had seen many curious and
wonderful things, he had not found anything marvelous enough to bring to the King.

Then one day, as he was going through a woods,
he was met by a large crowd of people, both men and
women, who warned him not to advance any farther
as he was entering the territory of the Snake-of-the-
Marvelous-Eye. The snake would devour him, they
said, for with his one marvelous eye he could see anyone who drew near his territory. The youth felt that
such a marvelous eye would, indeed, be the prize he
was searching for; so he told the people not to worry
about him, that he would fight and kill the Snake-of-
the-Marvelous-Eye. He pushed his way deeper into
the woods, but he had not gone far when he heard
the hissing of the snake. The youth, like his brothers,
was brave and unafraid, but he did climb onto a rock
that was surrounded by water. There, his sword in hand,
he awaited the snake.

It wasn't long in coming, but, since it had only one
eye, it could not tell which was the young man
and which was his reflection in the water. The youth
began to fight at once and cut away at the snake until
he had killed him. Then he cut off the head, and with
the point of his sword he lifted the eye from the snake's
forehead. It was like a crystal lens with which one
could see everything at any distance. He was overjoyed, for he knew that this was indeed the marvelous

thing to bring to the King; so he set out for the place where the brothers were to meet.

In the meantime, the youngest brother had taken the right-hand fork in the road. He had reached a land of yellow-skinned people, and there he had seen many rare and curious things; but he had not yet found anything marvelous enough to bring to the King. He was worried, for he saw that there was little time left for the search before he would have to return to his brothers. One day as he was walking through the high mountains, he came upon an old man who was dying. Although the youth was pushed for time, he did not want to leave the old man there alone, so he stayed and fed him and talked with him about God. The old man grew fond of the youth and told him that he was going to reveal the secret of his life. He was one hundred years old, he said, and he had been looking all his life for the Tree of Marvelous Fruit. He knew now where it was, but since he could not get there with only a few hours of life left to him, he was going to tell the secret so that the youth might succeed where he had failed. At the top of the highest mountain there was a cave, and in the cave there was a clearing, and that was where the Tree of Marvelous Fruit stood blooming. He who tasted that fruit would be cured, no matter how serious his illness might be. The cave was guarded by a ferocious eagle, the old man said, that caught anyone who came near in its claws and carried him off to its nest in the Tree of Marvelous Fruit as food for the baby eagles. When he finished his story, the old man died, and the youth grieved for him and buried him on the side of the road. Then he climbed up the mountain to the cave where the tree grew.

As he drew near the cave, he shot two deer. One of them he cleaned so that he could hide in its skin; the other he opened and filled with stones. In the morning, before the sun rose, he hid in the deer's body and waited for the eagle. It wasn't long before he heard a screech, and through a hole in the skin, he watched the eagle soar above the two deer. Not long afterward, he felt himself being lifted through the air as the eagle carried him to the top of the Tree of Marvelous Fruit. The eagle left the deer's body there, and the eaglets began picking away at it. The youth knew that the eagle had gone to get the other deer. He came out of the deerskin and quickly killed the eaglets with his sword. Then he climbed down through the branches until he came to the marvelous fruit itself. The fruit was like golden pears, but much larger. The youth took one; then, very quietly, so as not to attract the eagle's attention, he climbed out of the tree. The eagle was trying with all his might to lift the body of the other deer; but the stones with which the youth had filled it were so heavy that he could not move it. So the youth escaped with the marvelous fruit while the eagle struggled with the deer's body. He ran to where he had left his horse, and knowing that there was little time left to keep the appointment with his brothers, he rode at breakneck speed to the fork in the road where he was to meet them.

The eldest brother with his magic carpet and the middle brother with his magic crystal had both been waiting for him. On the last day of the time they had set for the meeting, both were very sad, for their youngest brother had not come and they feared some misfortune had befallen him. But at the last minute, they saw him coming. Half dead he was, too, from the arduous ride he had had.

The three brothers were very fond of each other and rejoiced to be together again. Then each one told of his adventures and showed the marvelous thing he had found to bring to the King. Each one thought that his gift would win the Princess whom they all loved.

They were so anxious to see the Princess that, before leaving for the King's castle, they decided to look through the magic crystal, which the middle brother had brought, to find out how she was. When they looked, they discovered that everyone in the castle was crying and that the Princess lay in her bed, dying.

The young men were heartbroken; but then the youngest brother reminded them of his marvelous fruit that could save the Princess's life if they could reach her in time. The eldest brother said they could do that if they rode on his magic carpet. It would transport them instantly to the castle and the Princess.

All three, with their marvelous things, sat on the carpet, which rose through the air, and in a few minutes reached the King's castle. Everyone there was happy to see them, but they were told about the Princess's illness and the fact that she might die at any moment. The three brothers ran up the castle stairs and told the King that one of their marvelous things would cure the Princess. The King led them to the Princess's bedroom, where she lay very ill. When the King told her that the three brothers had returned and were there, the Princess recovered enough to open her eyes a little, but tears came, for she knew she had to die. Then the King put the marvelous fruit to her lips and told her to bite into it. She managed to do so, and, immediately, the color came back into her cheeks, and

she opened her eyes again and smiled at the brothers. It was not long before she sat up in bed and laughed joyfully.

The news of the Princess's recovery brought joy to the whole castle, and everyone celebrated. The only one who remained quiet and thoughtful was the King. In spite of his great happiness at his daughter's recovery, he had a grave problem that he could not solve. He had given his promise that his daughter should marry the one who brought him the most marvelous thing, and all the brothers had brought marvelous things! To which one should he give his daughter?

The King called his wise counselors together to help him resolve the problem. Some of the counselors thought that the Princess belonged to the youngest brother, for he had brought the marvelous fruit that had cured

her. Others judged that the Princess should marry the middle brother, because it was he, with his magic crystal, who had discovered the Princess was dying, and the magic fruit would have been of no use had they not known she needed it. Other counselors thought that the Princess should marry the eldest brother because, had it not been for his magic carpet, they would not have arrived in time to save her, and neither knowledge of her illness nor the cure for it would have been of any use in saving her had they not arrived in time.

The King's counselors and the people were divided into these three factions, and each one thought the Princess ought to marry one of the brothers. No one ever knew which one of the three she did marry. If you had been the King, which one would you have chosen?

The Bird of Seven Colors

(EL PAJARO DE SIETE COLORES)

There was a mother who had two daughters. The elder, who resembled her mother, she loved very much, but she did not care for the younger daughter. One day she sent the younger daughter to the fountain for water, and on the way the girl dropped the water pitcher and it broke. The mother was furious. To punish her daughter, she sent her from home to look for the Bird of Seven Colors who would mend the pitcher, and she told her daughter that she could not come home again until the pitcher was mended.

The unhappy girl set out without knowing which way to go to find the Bird of Seven Colors. As she passed a mango tree, it spoke to her and asked where she was going. She said she was looking for the Bird of Seven Colors.

Then the tree said, "When you find him, ask him why I, who am so big and leafy, give no fruit."

The girl promised that she would and continued walking until she came to the seashore. When the sea saw her, it asked where she was going, and she told it she was going in search of the Bird of Seven Colors.

The sea said, "When you find him, ask him why my waters, so vast and deep, hold no fish."

The girl promised she would; then she went on until she reached the King's house. The King's daughters asked her where she was going, and she told them her story. They asked her, if she found the Bird of Seven Colors, to ask him why they, being so beautiful, had no children. The girl promised she would, and went on her way in search of the bird.

Finally, she reached an enchanted mountain where the Bird of Seven Colors lived with the little old woman who was his mother. When the mother of the Bird of Seven Colors saw the girl, she asked what she was doing there, and the girl told her story again. The little old woman said that she would help her, but that she must hide, for her son was wicked, and if he saw her there, he would eat her. So that the Bird of Seven Colors would not see the girl when he came home, his mother hid her in a barrel.

It wasn't long before the Bird of Seven Colors arrived and said to the little old woman, "Mother, the human smell is here; if you do not give it to me, I shall eat *you!*" The little old woman told him it was cow meat he smelled, and she gave him a piece of beef, which he gobbled up. Then he lay down and went to sleep.

When the bird was in bed, the mother called, "Birdling! Birdling!" and the bird asked what she wanted. She said that she had broken a pitcher and wondered

if he could fix it. He did, in no time at all, and went back to bed. It wasn't long before the mother called again, "Birdling! Birdling!"

He woke up and asked, "What is the matter, Mother?" The little old woman said that she had been dreaming about a very great mango tree, with luxuriant foliage, that bore no fruit. The Bird of Seven Colors told her that was because there was a treasure buried among its roots and, until the treasure was dug up, the tree would bear no fruit. The girl heard everything from her hiding place in the barrel and rejoiced to have the answer to the mango tree's question.

In the morning the bird left, and the little old woman took the girl out of the barrel and gave her something to eat and told her that that night she would ask two other questions.

As usual, the Bird of Seven Colors came home famished. He sniffed and said:

> "There's a smell of food;
> It is human, too;
> Give me human food,
> Or I shall eat *you!*"

The little old woman told him that it was the pork she had prepared for him which he smelled, and she gave some to the Bird of Seven Colors, who gobbled it up and went to bed. When he was asleep, the little old woman called, "Birdling! Birdling!" The bird woke up and asked what she wanted. The little old woman said why was it that a great, deep sea might not have fish in its waters.

The bird grumbled, sleepily, "It has to swallow someone before it can have fish," and went back to sleep.

It wasn't long before the little old woman called again, "Birdling! Birdling!" The Bird of Seven Colors grew furious. He sat up in bed and told her that if she didn't let him sleep, he would eat her! The little old woman said that she had been dreaming about the King's daughters who were very beautiful but had no children.

The angry bird snapped at his mother, "They'll have no children until they stop gazing at the moon!" and he went back to sleep.

The girl was overjoyed, for now her pitcher was mended and she knew the answers to the questions that had been asked her. In the morning, after the Bird of Seven Colors left, the little old woman took her out of the barrel, gave her something to eat, and said, "Now that you have what you came for, go, before my son returns!"

The grateful girl kissed the little old woman who had done so much for her and went home along the same road by which she had come. When she reached the King's house, his daughters asked her if she had the answer to their question. "Yes, I have," she answered, and she told them what the Bird of Seven Colors had said. The King's daughters were so pleased that they gave her many pretty clothes and pieces of jewelry.

When she came to the sea, it asked her if she had the answer to its question. "Yes, I have. Wait a minute, and I'll tell you," and she turned around and walked far, far from the shore, then called back, "The Bird of Seven Colors says that, in order to have fish, you must swallow someone." Then she ran away as fast as she could, for she knew that the sea is treacherous and would try to swallow her. The sea reached out a great, long wave, trying to catch her, but she was too far away, so the angry sea had to wait for someone else to swallow.

After walking a long time, the girl reached the mango tree and told it what the Bird of Seven Colors had said. Then the tree begged her to dig at its roots and remove the treasure. She did, and she found enough gold coins to fill her pitcher. The tree was very happy, knowing that now it could bear fruit.

After she left the tree, it did not take her long to reach home. Her mother was very surprised when she saw her dressed in pretty clothes, and even more surprised when she saw the mended pitcher filled with gold coins. The girl told her everything. Immediately, the vain woman set out for the house of the Bird of Seven Colors to see if there was another treasure hidden somewhere. She was thinking so hard about the riches she would find that she forgot what her daughter had said about the sea, and as she passed by on the shore, it reached out a great, long wave, pulled her in, and swallowed her.

Juan Bobo, the Sow, and the Chicks

(JUAN BOBO, EL PUERCO, Y LOS POLLOS)

Well, sir, once upon a time, in a long-ago town, there lived a widow and her son Juan. As the boy did strange things and was a bit of a fool, people called him Simple John, or *Juan Bobo*.

One day Juan Bobo's mother told him that she was going to church to hear Mass and that he was to take care of the animals while she was gone. Juan Bobo said she was not to worry, that he would take good care of them.

A little while after his mother had left, their sow began to groan. Juan Bobo thought that she wanted to go to church with his mother, so he said to her, "So you, too, want to hear Mass? Well, I'll send you to church, but you must be dressed properly for it."

Juan Bobo brought the sow into the house and dressed her in one of his mother's best suits; he tied a mantilla about her head and hung his mother's golden earrings on her ears and fastened beads around her neck.

When the sow was all dressed, he took her out and said, "There! Now you may go to church and come home with Mother."

As soon as he let her go, the sow ran to the mud puddle, threw herself in, and wriggled and scraped about in the muddy stones, trying to rub off the clothing and the jewelry.

Juan Bobo had gone back into the house and did not see what the sow was doing. Not long afterwards he heard the chicks peeping and said to them, "And now you! What do you want? To sleep up in the tree?"

Thinking that the chicks wanted to climb the tree and were crying because they couldn't, Juan Bobo took a pointed stick, strung all the chicks on it like beads, then hung the stick on a branch of the tree. As the chicks were dead, they didn't cry any more, and he thought that they had gone to sleep and was very pleased and proud of himself for the way he had taken care of them.

When his mother came home from church, she missed the sow and asked Juan Bobo where she was.

"As soon as you left, she began crying to go to Mass, and I dressed her in your clothes and jewelry and sent her off. Didn't you see her?" he explained.

Hearing this, Juan Bobo's mother ran to look for her sow and found her rolling in the mud, trying to rub off the last remnants of clothing that still stuck to her. His mother tied up the sow and brought it home. On the way, she noticed that the chicks were missing and asked Juan Bobo what he had done with *them*.

"Why, the chicks wanted to sleep in the tree, but they couldn't climb up, so I stuck them on a sharp stick and fastened them in the tree so that they wouldn't fall out."

His mother, suspecting the worst, went out to see and found all the chicks dead, strung up in the tree on a stick.

That day Juan Bobo received a whipping that he still remembers.

The Woodsman's Daughter
and the Lion

(LA HIJA DEL LEÑADOR Y EL LEÓN)

There was once a woodsman who went every day to the forest to cut wood. One day while he was chopping down a tree, a great, ferocious lion appeared, and the woodsman, fearing for his life, threw himself upon his knees and begged the lion not to eat him, explaining that he was a poor woodsman who had to work hard to take care of his three daughters.

Hearing this, the lion said, "Very well, I shall not eat you, but you must make a promise to me." The woodsman was pleased at this and agreed to promise whatever the lion asked.

Then the lion said, "I shall not eat you if you promise to bring me tomorrow the first thing that comes to receive you when you get home this afternoon."

The woodsman was even more pleased at this, thinking how easily he had saved his life, for it was his little dog that always ran out to greet him. So he made the promise.

That afternoon the woodsman gathered the wood he had cut and set off for home, feeling very lucky. But his happiness changed to sorrow as he neared home when, instead of the little dog that usually greeted him, he saw his youngest daughter run out. She threw her arms about him. The unhappy woodsman asked her what had happened to the little dog, and she said that the dog had a thorn in his paw, and they had kept it indoors.

When he went into the house, all of his daughters noticed their father's sadness and asked him what had happened to make him so unhappy. The woodsman, crying, told them about his promise to the lion and how he must take his youngest daughter to the lion tomorrow. He loved her very much, but he must keep his word. He could not break the pact he had made with the lion. He didn't know what to do!

The youngest daughter, who loved her father more than the other two did, told him not to worry, that she wasn't afraid to go with him tomorrow to meet the lion.

The next morning the woodsman and his daughter set out. When they reached the place in the forest where the lion had appeared the day before, there he was, waiting for them. The woodsman begged the lion to release him from the pact because he loved his daughter so much that he could not bear to lose her. The lion reminded him of his promise, then turned to the young girl and said, "Follow me." But before leaving, he told the woodsman to dig beneath a tree nearby, and he would find gold at its roots. Then the lion entered a cave, and the young girl followed

him, leaving her father alone and in tears. After they had gone, the woodsman remembered what the lion had told him, and he dug beneath the tree and found many golden coins. He took them home and now, with so much money, he and his other daughters lived without having to work so hard.

Meantime, the youngest daughter had come with the lion to an underground palace. There she found many beautiful dresses, jewelry, and all the lovely things she had dreamed of awaiting her. The lion was very kind and gave her anything she asked for. Months passed, and the young girl grew very unhappy because she missed her family. One day the lion asked what was troubling her, and she told him that she was sad because she had not seen her sisters or her father for such a long time. So the lion told her that the next day she might visit them, but that she must return before the rooster crowed. This made her happy again, and the next morning, when she left the cave, there stood a carriage ready to take her to her parent's house. At home, everyone was pleased to see that nothing had happened to her and to hear how happily she was living and how kind the lion was to her.

Before the rooster crowed at sunrise the young girl said good-by to her father and sisters and stepped into the carriage to return to the enchanted palace.

More months passed, and again the girl grew sad, so the lion told her to visit her home once more, reminding her to return before the rooster crowed. Happily she stepped into the carriage to go to her father's house. When she arrived, she found that her father was ill. She gave him his medicine and cared for him. But she was so preoccupied with his illness that she did not notice the sun had risen and the roosters were crowing to announce a new day. When she realized what had happened, she was frightened, said goodby to her father and her sisters at once, and hurried out to the carriage that had brought her. It was nowhere to be seen! Very upset about having broken her promise to the lion, she walked to the woods and came to the tree where she had first met him. There was nothing there. She continued walking and came to the entrance of the cave, but it was sealed up. She sat down and cried. As she sat there, she heard the voice of the lion telling her that she had broken her promise to him and that he was a prince who had been bewitched. She had *almost* broken the evil spell that bound him; but now she would have to walk across the world and wear out a pair of iron shoes before she could find him again to break the spell and set him free.

Through her tears, the girl promised that she would do this. She went to the blacksmith and had him make her a pair of iron shoes; she put them on and began walking across the world in search of the lion.

Many years passed in the search. When the iron soles of her shoes were worn as thin as a sheet of paper, she reached the house of the sun. She asked the sun's mother if she knew where the lion was. She didn't know, but said to ask her son when he returned. It wasn't long before a great heat was felt, and the sun arrived. His mother asked him if he knew where the enchanted lion was, and he said, no, he didn't; but perhaps the moon would know. The young girl said good-by to them and went on to find the moon's house. When she arrived, the moon's mother said that her daughter had not come home yet, but to wait and she would ask her. Then the girl felt a chill, and the moon arrived. When the mother asked if she knew where the enchanted lion was, the moon answered that she had seen him at night in a castle behind a great mountain. The young girl left that very day for the mountain. After walking across the mountain without stopping to rest, she came to a castle with great doors, which were all locked. She knocked and knocked at one of the doors, but no one opened it. In desperation, she pulled off one of her iron shoes and threw it at the door. Instantly, all the doors flew open and, as though by magic, a handsome prince appeared and took her in his arms, explaining that he was the lion who, thanks to her love and loyalty, had been freed from the evil spell a witch had cast upon him.

The young girl was filled with joy and lived happily with the prince, and her father and sisters came to live with them as well.

The Ant in Search of Her Leg

(LA HORMIGUITA EN BUSCA DE SU PATITA)

Once upon a time, in a very cold country, there lived a little ant. One snowy day when the little ant left her hole to search for food, one of her feet froze to the snow, and she pulled so hard to free it that she pulled it off.

When the little ant saw what had happened, she was very sad, and she went to snow and said, "Snow, you who are so strong, give back my little leg."

Snow answered, "Sun is stronger than I. It melts me."

So the little ant went to Sun and said, "Sun, so strong that melts Snow, tell it to give back my little leg."

Sun answered, "Cloud is stronger than I. It covers me."

So the little ant went to Cloud and said, "Cloud, so strong that covers Sun that melts Snow, tell it to give back my little leg."

Cloud answered, "Wind is stronger than I. It moves me."

So the little ant went to Wind and said, "Wind, so strong that moves Cloud that covers Sun that melts Snow, tell it to give back my little leg."

Wind answered, "Wall is stronger than I. It stops me."

So the little ant went to Wall and said, "Wall, so strong that stops Wind that moves Cloud that covers Sun that melts Snow, tell it to give back my little leg."

Wall answered, "Rat is stronger than I. It gnaws me."

So the little ant went to Rat and said, "Rat, so strong that gnaws Wall that stops Wind that moves Cloud that covers Sun that melts Snow, tell it to give back my little leg."

Rat answered, "Cat is stronger than I. It eats me."

So the little ant went to Cat and said, "Cat, so strong that eats Rat that gnaws Wall that stops Wind that moves Cloud that covers Sun that melts Snow, tell it to give back my little leg."

Cat answered, "Dog is stronger than I. It chases me."

So the little ant went to Dog and said, "Dog, so strong that chases Cat that eats Rat that gnaws Wall that stops Wind that moves Cloud that covers Sun that melts Snow, tell it to give back my little leg."

Dog answered, "Stick is stronger than I. It beats me."

So the little ant went to Stick and said, "Stick, so strong that beats Dog that chases Cat that eats Rat that gnaws Wall that stops Wind that moves Cloud that covers Sun that melts Snow, tell it to give back my little leg."

Stick answered, "Fire is stronger than I. It burns me."

So the little ant went to Fire and said, "Fire, so strong that burns Stick that beats Dog that chases Cat that eats Rat that gnaws Wall that stops Wind that moves Cloud that covers Sun that melts Snow, tell it to give back my little leg."

Fire answered, "Water is stronger than I. It puts me out."

So the little ant went to Water and said, "Water, so strong that puts out Fire that burns Stick that beats Dog that chases Cat that eats Rat that gnaws Wall that stops Wind that moves Cloud that covers Sun that melts Snow, tell it to give back my little leg."

Water answered, "Ox is stronger than I. It drinks me."

So the little ant went to Ox and said, "Ox, so strong that drinks Water that puts out Fire that burns Stick that beats Dog that chases Cat that eats Rat that gnaws Wall that stops Wind that moves Cloud that covers Sun that melts Snow, tell it to give back my little leg."

Ox answered, "Knife is stronger than I. It kills me."

So the little ant went to Knife and said, "Knife, so strong that kills Ox that drinks Water that puts out Fire that burns Stick that beats Dog that chases Cat that eats Rat that gnaws Wall that stops Wind that moves Cloud that covers Sun that melts Snow, tell it to give back my little leg."

Knife said, "Man is stronger than I. He makes me."

So the little ant went to Man and said, "Man, so

strong that makes Knife that kills Ox that drinks Water that puts out Fire that burns Stick that beats Dog that chases Cat that eats Rat that gnaws Wall that stops Wind that moves Cloud that covers Sun that melts Snow, tell it to give back my little leg."

Man answered, "Death is stronger than I. It takes me."

So the little ant went to Death and said, "Death, so strong that takes Man that makes Knife that kills Ox that drinks Water that puts out Fire that burns Stick that beats Dog that chases Cat that eats Rat that gnaws Wall that stops Wind that moves Cloud that covers Sun that melts Snow, tell it to give back my little leg."

Death answered, "God is stronger than I. He commands me."

So the little ant went to God and said, "God, so strong that commands Death that takes Man that makes Knife that kills Ox that drinks Water that puts out Fire that burns Stick that beats Dog that chases Cat that eats Rat that gnaws Wall that stops Wind that moves Cloud that covers Sun that melts Snow, tell it to give back my little leg."

God answered, "Little ant, go home. When you leave it again, you will have your leg." The little ant went home happily, having learned that God is the strongest of all.

The Rabbit and the Tiger

(EL CONEJO Y EL TIGRE)

Once upon a time there were two great friends—a rabbit and a tiger. The rabbit, who was much quicker than the tiger, was forever playing tricks upon his friend; and the tiger was forever chasing the rabbit to eat him. So, they were great friends.

One day, when the rabbit had nothing to eat, he remembered that this was the day when his friend the tiger took the cheese he had made to the market. The rabbit was very hungry and decided he would eat the tiger's cheese. He went to the road he knew the tiger would take and stretched out upon it as though he were dead. The tiger came along and saw him.

"A dead rabbit. I'll pick it up to eat on my way back," he said, and went on to the market. As soon as he had gone, the rabbit jumped up and hurried by way of a shortcut he knew to a place farther along the road. There he lay down again and pretended to be dead. When the tiger came to the spot and saw the rabbit lying there, he said, "Another dead rabbit! With this and the first one I saw, I'll have a fine meal!" Although his appetite increased with the thought of the rabbit dish he would make, the tiger decided to go on to the market with his cheese. As soon as he had passed, the rabbit jumped off a ledge and landed below, just in the turning of the road that the tiger would have to pass. Again he stretched out and pretended to be dead. The tiger came along dreaming of the fine rabbit stew he was going to enjoy, and when he saw the rabbit on the road—it was too much!

"I'm going to eat these rabbits now!" he exclaimed. He threw down his cheeses and hurried back to collect the other two he had seen.

As soon as he left, the rabbit jumped up, collected the cheeses, and ran off with them to hide from the tiger and eat in peace.

The tiger searched and searched, but he did not find a single dead rabbit; but he did begin to suspect his friend of playing tricks. He lost no time in hurrying back to rescue his cheeses. But he found neither rabbit nor cheeses. He was furious and set out to find the rabbit so that he could kill and eat him!

After looking a long time, the tiger saw the rabbit on the side of a hill. The rabbit had eaten all the cheeses and was resting. When he saw the tiger coming, he knew there was no escape. He got up and braced himself against a great rock, as though he were holding it on the hill.

The tiger came, ready to eat him, but when he saw that the rabbit did not run away but stood fast against the rock, he asked, "My friend, what is the matter? Why are you huddled against that rock?"

The rabbit, who was expecting this question, answered, "Ay, my friend, help me hold this rock! It is rolling down, and if it falls all the way, the world will end!"

The tiger grew very frightened at these words and braced himself against the rock. The rabbit told him to hold fast while he went for help. He said that he would return with other animals, and he ran off, laughing at the tiger. The tiger stayed there many hours until his strength gave out and he let go. To his surprise, nothing happened; the stone didn't move. When he realized that he had been fooled again by his friend the rabbit, he was furious and set off to find him.

He knew how quick the rabbit was and decided to see if he could catch his sly friend with one of his own tricks. He hid in the rabbit's house, hoping to catch him and eat him when he came home.

But the rabbit was suspicious and ready for him. As he drew near his house, he called out, "My house, my house, how are things in my house?"

The tiger heard him but kept still.

Then the rabbit said, in a louder voice, "My goodness! Something is the matter with my house; someone must be in it, or it would answer me," and he called again.

"My house, my house, how are things in my house?"

The tiger, who was stupid enough to believe all that he heard, tried to disguise his voice and answered, "Come in, rabbit, come in. No one is here."

The rabbit recognized the tiger's voice, laughed, and said, "Houses don't talk, stupid!" Then he ran as fast as he could and hid in the woods. The tiger saw that he had been stupid in telling the rabbit he wasn't there, and, angrier than ever, he swore he'd get even with his friend.

One day when the rabbit was fishing in the river, the tiger came along and said, "You won't escape me this time."

The rabbit smiled and answered, "Ah, my friend, you have come at a bad time. I was about to pull a big cheese out of the river, and now you're going to eat me."

The tiger, who was a glutton, no sooner heard the word "cheese" than his mouth began to water, and he asked the rabbit where it was. The rabbit pointed to a great bundle lying on the river bed. The tiger said he would get it and eat it with the rabbit stew he was going to have. The rabbit said that that was a good idea, to jump in and get the cheese, but in order to reach the bottom of the river, he'd better tie himself to a big stone. So the tiger, thinking only of the cheese he was going to get, tied a big stone to his tail and jumped into the river. When he reached the bottom, he found that the rabbit had fooled him again.

What he had seen and believed to be cheese was nothing but the reflection of the moon on the water. The rabbit stood on the river bank laughing uproariously at the stupidity of his friend who by now was on the point of drowning. He barely managed to pull himself out of the river, and by then the rabbit was nowhere to be seen.

Some time passed, and the tiger continued to be annoyed with the rabbit. He looked everywhere for him, to kill him and eat him. Then, one day while the rabbit was gathering vines with which to make ropes, the tiger came along and said, "Now, nothing can save you, my friend. I'm going to eat you this time!"

The rabbit saw that he was lost; the tiger was too near; there was no escape, so he said, "Ah, my friend, what a shame you chose today for eating me. You see, there is a great storm approaching, and I am gathering vines to tie myself down so that the wind won't blow me away."

The tiger knew what a hurricane could do and became frightened. He cried to the rabbit, "Give me those vines! Tie me tightly to the tree so that I won't be blown away!"

The rabbit used all the vines and tied the tiger to the tree, and when he was sure he could not get loose, he said to him, "My friend, here comes the hurricane!" and, picking up a switch, he began beating the tiger, who shouted and swore that he was being killed. He also knew he was being made a fool of! The rabbit went off and left the tiger abandoned there for several days until he managed to get free himself. He reached home half dead.

The rabbit boasted to everyone about what he had done, and he made a bet that he could ride the tiger through the streets of the town as though he were a horse.

First he sent a letter to the tiger saying that he was sick and most sorry and apologetic for all the tricks he had played and that he wanted the tiger to come and eat him. When the tiger received the letter, he thought that at last his problems were ended, and he went to his friend's house. When the rabbit saw him coming, he got in bed and pretended to be sick. "Aye, my friend!" He sighed as the tiger leaned over him. "I'm so sick! Please eat me so that I can repay you for all the grief I have caused."

The tiger said that was all very well, but he could not eat a sick rabbit because he might be poisoned or the disease might be contagious.

Then the rabbit, who knew this was how the tiger would feel, said, "My friend, carry me to your house, and you can eat me when I am better." The tiger said this was a good idea and would the rabbit please get up and come home with him. The rabbit made an effort to rise, then fell back and sighed. "Aye, my friend,

I can't walk. You'll have to carry me on your back."
The tiger said that was fine and to get on his back. So
the rabbit climbed up, but he fell off again, saying,
"Aye, my friend, if I ride on your back, I'll need a
saddle." The tiger said that was all right, so the rabbit
put a saddle on his back and climbed up, but he fell
off again, saying, "Aye, my friend, I can't hold on without reins and a bit." The tiger answered that he didn't
like the idea, but to hurry up and get it over with.
The rabbit, chuckling to himself, fastened on the har-
ness and adjusted the bit in the tiger's mouth. Then
he climbed up, and as soon as he saw that all was
just right, he gave a jerk on the reins that sent the
tiger running through the town where everyone could
see the rabbit mounted on the tiger.

The tiger was so angry that he ran as though he
were crazy and wouldn't stop. So the rabbit jumped
off his back and hid among the rocks. Later he returned to town and collected the bets he had won
by riding the tiger.

The tiger still looks for the rabbit to kill and eat
him. But he hasn't found him to this day.

> And red, white, and blue,
> THE END—
> This is true!

Death's Godchild

(EL AHIJADO DE LA MUERTE)

There was once a woman who was very poor, with no one to turn to for help. She had a little son who was sick, and she was anxious to have him baptized before he died, but she could find no one to be his godparents.

One day a woman passed by dressed in black, and the poor mother asked her to serve as godmother at the baptism of her child. The woman consented, but they had to look for a godfather. A little while after this, a man with gold teeth came along and offered to be the godfather.

When the day came for the baptism, the man said that he could not enter the church, but he promised to be a good godfather, saying that he would teach the child the art of healing. So the boy was baptized, and he regained his health. As he grew older, his mother became aware that her child could cure sick people. His fame as a healer spread, and he made much money.

One day, when the boy was a grown man, his godmother appeared and told him that she was Death and that whenever he saw her at the head of a sick person's bed, he was not to make a cure, for she must have that person.

Not long after, the youth heard that the King's daughter was gravely ill and that the King had promised his crown to the person who could save her. The young man liked the idea of being king and marrying the Princess, so he presented himself at the palace and asked to be allowed to cure the Princess.

As he entered the Princess's room, he saw that his godmother, Death, stood at the head of the bed. The youth begged her to allow him to cure the Princess as he wanted so much to be king. His godmother told him it was no use, for within two days the Princess would die. Then she took him home with her and showed him the thousands of candles burning there and explained that each candle represented the life of a person. She showed him the Princess's candle, and it was nearly burned out. The youth was ambitious, having been influenced by his godfather, who was none other than the Devil himself. He determined to save the Princess in spite of everything. And he did—she became so well that she got out of bed and walked about the palace.

The King kept his word. When he saw that his daughter was healthy again, he gave his crown to the youth, bestowed many riches upon him, and married him to the Princess. Finding himself so rich, the youth

determined to take no chances on losing his fortune. As he knew that the Princess had only a few hours of life left, he went to his godmother's house to see if he could do something to keep her candle from burning out. While his godmother was not looking, he lifted the candle end that belonged to the Princess to light a new one with it. But since it was so short now, he burned his fingers and dropped it, and it fell upon another candle nearby and put it out.

At that very moment, the youth fell dead. He had dropped the Princess's candle on his own, causing his own death.

Perez and Martina

(LA CUCARACHA MARTINA Y EL RATONCITO PEREZ)

Once upon a time there was a little cockroach named Martina. One day when Martina was sweeping the floor, she found a coin, and the little cockroach sat down upon the lower step of her house to think what she would buy with it.

"If I buy bread, it won't last long;
If I buy salt, it won't last long;
If I buy sugar, it won't last long."

Then the little cockroach, who was very vain and something of a coquette, decided to buy powder with it. She bought the powder and dusted herself all over so that she was pretty and white. Then she sat on the front step to watch the passersby.

A bull came along, and seeing pretty Martina, said to her, "Little cockroach, Martina, will you marry me?"

The little cockroach asked, "And what do you do at night?"

"Muuu, muuu, muuu," answered the bull.

"Ay! No, no, you frighten me!" said the little cockroach, and the bull went away.

A little later a cat came along, and seeing the little cockroach, he said to her, "Little cockroach, Martina, will you marry me?"

The little cockroach asked, "And what do you do at night?"

"Miau, miau, miau," answered the cat.

"Ay! No, no, you frighten me!" said the little cockroach, and the cat went away.

And so the little cockroach refused all the animals who passed by.

Then came Perez, the mouse, and seeing the little cockroach, he said to her, "Little cockroach, Martina, would you like to marry me?"

The little cockroach asked him the same question, and Perez, the mouse, answered gently: "Chui, chui, chui."

"Ay! Yes, yes, I like that! I will marry you."

And so it was that the little cockroach, Martina, married Perez, the mouse, and they were very happy.

But one day, while the little cockroach was cooking one of Perez's special dishes, the mouse smelled it and climbed up to look into the big pot. He fell in and died. When the little cockroach returned and saw what had happened, she was very sad and began to cry and sing:

"Perez, the mouse, fell in the pot,
Little cockroach, Martina, sings
And cries for him . . ."

The Chili Plant

(LA MATA DE AJI)

A long time ago, in a distant country, there was a widower who had two children, a boy and a girl. The children were very little, and the man decided to marry again so that they would have a mother to care for them. As luck would have it, he chose for his wife an unkind woman who did not like children. As soon as she arrived, she began scolding them, especially the little girl who looked so much like her dead mother.

There was a fig tree at their house, and the stepmother would allow no one to pick a single fig from it. Each time she went out, she left the girl in charge of the tree, threatening to punish her severely if she ate a fig or allowed anybody to pick one.

One day, before she left the house, the stepmother counted the figs on the tree and reminded the girl that she would punish her if a single fig was missing when she returned.

That day the girl brought her sewing out and sat down beside the tree to guard it. She had been there several hours when a little old man came along and asked her for water, saying that he had come a long way and was thirsty. The girl asked him politely to wait there while she went into the kitchen to get a glass of water. While she was gone, the little old man, who was also very hungry, picked a fig from the tree and ate it. When the girl returned with the water, the little old man thanked her and blessed her, entrusting her soul to the Virgin's care. Then he went on his way.

She did not notice that he had picked a fig, and when her mother returned in the afternoon, the girl assured her in good faith that the tree was just as she had left it. The woman counted the figs and became very angry when she discovered that one was missing. She beat the girl and wanted to know what she had done with the missing fig. The girl cried out that she hadn't picked it, but this only made the woman more furious, so that her blows became harder. She grew so angry that she decided to rid herself of the girl at once and for all time. Pulling her to the edge of a hole in the garden, the stepmother threw a chili bean in and told the girl to reach down and pick it out. As the girl obediently leaned over to reach for the chili bean, her wicked stepmother pushed her in and filled the hole with dirt.

That evening, when the children's father returned and asked for his daughter, the stepmother told him that the girl had gone to visit her aunt and that she would stay with her for quite some time.

Days and days passed, and out in the garden, over the hole into which the wicked stepmother had pushed the girl, a sprout of chili plant appeared. The plant grew and produced many chilis.

One day, as they were seated at the table, the father, who felt very unhappy about his daughter's long absence, wanted a chili. He sent his son to the garden to get one. The boy went to the plant and picked a chili. As he did so, he was startled to hear a voice, which resembled his sister's, sing:

> "Brother, my brother,
> Do not pull my hair;
> For want of a fig,
> My wicked stepmother
> Buried me here."

The frightened boy ran to his father and told him what had happened out at the chili plant and repeated the words of the song he had heard. The father was so horrified that he could not believe what his son had said. He hurried out to the chili plant, pulled off a chili, and heard the voice of his daughter sing:

> "Father, my father,
> Do not pull my hair;
> For want of a fig,
> My wicked stepmother
> Buried me here."

The father recognized his daughter's voice, and in great anger he returned for his wife. He dragged her to the plant and forced her to pick a chili. The moment she did, the voice of the girl came clearly:

"Oh, my stepmother,
　　Do not pull my hair;
　　For want of a fig,
　　You buried me here."

The frightened woman was so shocked and filled with such remorse for what she had done that she fell

down dead, beside the plant. The father and his son
began to dig. At the bottom of the hole, they found
the girl, alive and well. The Virgin had protected her.
The father and his two children lived happily ever after.

"Red, white and blue,
The story's ended. True!"

The Plumage of the Owl

(EL PLUMAJE DEL MUCARO)

A long time ago, the animals used to give parties and balls and have good times together. At this time the birds decided to give a ball, and they invited all the bird family to come. The hawk was in charge of issuing the invitations, and he called upon each bird to invite him personally.

When he came to the owl's house, he found him naked. The owl told him that he could not come to the ball as he had no clothes to wear. The hawk told the other birds about this, and they decided that each one of them would lend the owl a feather so that he could make a dress suit and come to the ball.

The hawk collected feathers of different colors from each and took them to the owl but told him that, after the ball was over, each feather was to be returned to its owner. The owl was delighted with the feathers. He made himself a fine dress suit and appeared at the ball.

But the owl was very vain, and so pleased was he with the suit of many colors that he could hardly enjoy the ball for thinking of how he would be naked again after it ended, when he had to return all the fine feathers. When no one was looking, he left the ball and hid in the forest.

The other birds are still looking for him; they want their feathers back. And this is why the owl is never seen by day, only at night when the other birds are sleeping.

Lazy Peter and
His Three-Cornered Hat

(PEDRO ANIMALA Y
SU SOMBRERO DE TRES PICOS)

This is the story of Lazy Peter, a shameless rascal of a fellow who went from village to village making mischief.

One day Lazy Peter learned that a fair was being held in a certain village. He knew that a large crowd of country people would be there selling horses, cows, and other farm animals and that a large amount of money would change hands. Peter, as usual, needed money, but it was not his custom to work for it. So he set out for the village, wearing a red three-cornered hat.

The first thing he did was to stop at a stand and leave a big bag of money with the owner, asking him to keep it safely until he returned for it. Peter told the man that when he returned for the bag of money, one corner of his hat would be turned down, and that was how the owner of the stand would know him. The man promised to do this, and Peter thanked him. Then he went to the drugstore in the village and gave the druggist another bag of money, asking him to keep it until he returned with one corner of his hat turned up. The druggist agreed, and Peter left. He went to the church and asked the priest to keep another bag of money and to return it to him only when he came back with one corner of his hat twisted to the side. The priest said fine, that he would do this.

Having disposed of three bags of money, Peter went to the edge of the village where the farmers were buying and selling horses and cattle. He stood and watched for a while until he decided that one of the farmers must be very rich indeed, for he had sold all of his horses and cows. Moreover, the man seemed to be a miser who was never satisfied but wanted always more and more money. This was Peter's man! He stopped beside him. It was raining; and instead of keeping his hat on to protect his head, he took it off and wrapped it carefully in his cape, as though it were very valuable. It puzzled the farmer to see Peter stand there with the rain falling on his head and his hat wrapped in his cape.

After a while he asked, "Why do you take better care of your hat than of your head?"

Peter saw that the farmer had swallowed the bait, and smiling to himself, he said that the hat was the most valuable thing in all the world and that was why he took care to protect it from the rain. The farmer's curiosity increased at this reply, and he asked Peter what was so valuable about a red three-cornered hat. Peter told him that the hat worked for him; thanks to it, he never had to work for a living because, whenever he put the hat on with one of the corners turned over, people just handed him any money he asked for.

The farmer was amazed and very interested in what Peter said. As money-getting was his greatest ambition, he told Peter that he couldn't believe a word of it until he saw the hat work with his own eyes. Peter assured him that he could do this, for he, Peter, was hungry, and the hat was about to start working since he had no money with which to buy food.

With this, Peter took out his three-cornered hat, turned one corner down, put it on his head, and told the farmer to come along and watch the hat work. Peter took the farmer to the stand. The minute the owner looked up, he handed over the bag of money Peter had left with him. The farmer stood with his mouth open in astonishment. He didn't know what to make of it. But of one thing he was sure—he had to have that hat!

Peter smiled and asked if he was satisfied, and the farmer said, yes, he was. Then he asked Peter if he would sell the hat. This was just what Lazy Peter wanted, but he said no, that he was not interested in selling the hat because, with it, he never had to work and he always had money. The farmer said he thought that was unsound reasoning because thieves could easily steal a hat, and wouldn't it be safer to invest in a

farm with cattle? So they talked, and Peter pretended
to be impressed with the farmer's arguments. Finally
he said yes, that he saw the point, and if the farmer
would make him a good offer, he would sell the hat.
The farmer, who had made up his mind to have the
hat at any price, offered a thousand pesos. Peter laughed
aloud and said he could make as much as that by just
putting his hat on two or three times.

As they continued haggling over the price, the
farmer grew more and more determined to have that
hat until, finally, he offered all he had realized from
the sale of his horses and cows—ten thousand pesos in
gold. Peter still pretended not to be interested, but he
chuckled to himself, thinking of the trick he was about
to play on the farmer. All right, he said, it was a deal.
Then the farmer grew cautious and told Peter that,
before he handed over the ten thousand pesos, he would
like to see the hat work again. Peter said that was
fair enough. He put on the hat with one of the corners
turned up and went with the farmer to the drugstore.
The moment the druggist saw the turned-up corner,
he handed over the money Peter had left with him. At
this the farmer was convinced and very eager to set
the hat to work for himself. He took out a bag con-
taining ten thousand pesos in gold and was about to
hand it to Peter when he had a change of heart and
thought better of it. He asked Peter please to excuse
him, but he had to see the hat work just once more

before he could part with his gold. Peter said that that
was fair enough, but now he would have to ask the
farmer to give him the fine horse he was riding as well
as the ten thousand pesos in gold. The farmer's interest
in the hat revived, and he said it was a bargain!

Lazy Peter put on his hat again, doubled over one of
the corners, and told the farmer that, since he still
seemed to have doubts, this time he could watch the
hat work in the church. The farmer was delighted
with this, his doubts were stilled, and he fairly beamed
thinking of all the money he was going to make once
that hat was his.

They entered the church. The priest was hearing
confession, but when he saw Peter with his hat, he
said, "Wait here, my son," and he went to the sacristy
and returned with the bag of money Peter had left
with him. Peter thanked the priest, then knelt and
asked for a blessing before he left. The farmer had
seen everything and was fully convinced of the hat's
magic powers. As soon as they left the church, he gave
Peter the ten thousand pesos in gold and told him to
take the horse, also. Peter tied the bag of pesos to
the saddle, gave the hat to the farmer, begging him to
take good care of it, spurred his horse, and galloped
out of town.

As soon as he was alone, the farmer burst out laughing at the thought of the trick he had played on Lazy
Peter. A hat such as this was priceless! He couldn't

wait to try it. He put it on with one corner turned up and entered the butcher shop. The butcher looked at the hat, which was very handsome, indeed, but said nothing. The farmer turned around, then walked up and down until the butcher asked him what he wanted. The farmer said he was waiting for the bag of money. The butcher laughed aloud and asked if he was crazy. The farmer thought that there must be something wrong with the way he had folded the hat. He took it off and doubled another corner down. But this had no effect on the butcher. So he decided to try it out some other place. He went to the Mayor of the town.

The Mayor, to be sure, looked at the hat but did nothing. The farmer grew desperate and decided to go to the druggist who had given Peter a bag of money. He entered and stood with the hat on. The druggist looked at him but did nothing.

The farmer became very nervous. He began to suspect that there was something very wrong. He shouted at the druggist, "Stop looking at me and hand over the bag of money!"

The druggist said he owed him nothing, and what bag of money was he talking about, anyway? As the farmer continued to shout about a bag of money and a magic hat, the druggist called the police. When they arrived, he told them that the farmer had gone out of his mind and kept demanding a bag of money. The police questioned the farmer, and he told them about the magic hat he had bought from Lazy Peter. When he heard the story, the druggist explained that Peter had left a bag of money, asking that it be returned when he appeared with a corner of his hat turned up. The owner of the stand and the priest told the same story. And I am telling you the farmer was so angry that he tore the hat to shreds and walked home.

Juan Bobo and the Caldron

(JUAN BOBO Y EL CALDERO)

There was once upon a time a widow with a son who was so stupid that people called him Juan Bobo or Simple John. One day his mother was preparing chicken and rice and found that she did not have a caldron big enough to hold the stew, so she sent her son to his grandmother's house to borrow one.

When Juan Bobo got to his grandmother's house, he said to her, "Mami sent me to borrow a big pot for making a stew of chicken and rice."

His grandmother went to the kitchen and brought back a great caldron, the old-fashioned kind with three little feet. Juan took the caldron and balanced it on his shoulders and started to walk home. After a while he grew tired, for the caldron was heavy. He set it down on the ground and studied it a while.

Then he said, "Why should I carry you, you loafer! You have three feet to walk with faster than I can. Get along the road, now! I'm going to take a shortcut. Let's see if your three feet can get you home to Mami before my two feet get me there!"

Juan Bobo ran as fast as he could to reach home. His mother was waiting at the door, and when she saw him coming without the caldron, she asked him what had happened. Why hadn't he brought it? Juan explained that, since the caldron had three feet, he had left it on the road to come home alone while he had taken the shortcut.

"Isn't it here yet, Mami?" he asked.

His mother gave him a thrashing and sent him back for the caldron.

The Three Wishes
(LOS TRES DESEOS)

Many years ago, in the days when the saints walked on earth, there lived a woodsman and his wife. They were very poor but very happy in their little house in the forest. Poor as they were, they were always ready to share what little they had with anyone who came to their door. They loved each other very much and were quite content with their life together. Each evening, before eating, they gave thanks to God for their happiness.

One day, while the husband was working far off in the woods, an old man came to the little house and said that he had lost his way in the forest and had eaten nothing for many days. The woodsman's wife had little to eat herself, but, as was her custom, she gave a large portion of it to the old man. After he had eaten everything she gave him, he told the woman that he had been sent by God to test her and that, as a reward for the kindness she and her husband showed to all who came to their house, they would be granted a special grace. This pleased the woman, and she asked what the special grace was.

The old man answered, "Beginning immediately, any three wishes you or your husband may wish will come true."

When she heard these words, the woman was overjoyed and exclaimed, "Oh, if my husband were only here to hear what you say!"

The last word had scarcely left her lips when the woodsman appeared in the little house with the ax still in his hands. The first wish had come true.

The woodsman couldn't understand it at all. How did it happen that he, who had been cutting wood in the forest, found himself here in his house? His wife explained it all as she embraced him. The woodsman just stood there, thinking over what his wife had said. He looked at the old man who stood quietly, too, saying nothing.

Suddenly he realized that his wife, without stopping to think, had used one of the three wishes, and he became very annoyed when he remembered all of the useful things she might have asked for with the first wish. For the first time, he became angry with his wife. The desire for riches had turned his head, and he scolded his wife, shouting at her, among other things, "It doesn't seem possible that you could be so stupid! You've wasted one of our wishes, and now we have only two left! May you grow ears of a donkey!"

He had no sooner said the words than his wife's ears

began to grow, and they continued to grow until they changed into the pointed, furry ears of a donkey.

When the woman put her hand up and felt them, she knew what had happened and began to cry. Her husband was very ashamed and sorry, indeed, for what he had done in his temper, and he went to his wife to comfort her.

The old man, who had stood by silently, now came to them and said, "Until now, you have known happiness together and have never quarreled with each other. Nevertheless, the mere knowledge that you

could have riches and power has changed you both. Remember, you have only one wish left. What do you want? Riches? Beautiful clothes? Servants? Power?"

The woodsman tightened his arm about his wife, looked at the old man, and said, "We want only the happiness and joy we knew before my wife grew donkey's ears."

No sooner had he said these words than the donkey ears disappeared. The woodsman and his wife fell upon their knees to ask God's forgiveness for having acted, if only for a moment, out of covetousness and greed. Then they gave thanks for all the happiness God had given them.

The old man left, but before going, he told them that they had undergone this test in order to learn that there can be happiness in poverty just as there can be unhappiness in riches. As a reward for their repentence, the old man said that he would bestow upon them the greatest happiness a married couple can know. Months later, a son was born to them. The family lived happily all the rest of their lives.

The Young Girl
and the Devil

(LA JOVEN Y EL DIABLO)

Once upon a time there was a beautiful girl who paid no attention to any of the young men in town. They all fell in love with her, but she disdained them all, for she felt none was worthy of her.

One day a well-dressed youth came to town riding upon a black horse, and when he saw the young girl, he smiled broadly, showing his teeth. All of them were of gold. The young girl, who was vain and foolish, was so impressed by the youth's gold teeth that she fell in love with him.

Her parents advised her against marrying the young man because he was a stranger and unknown to them. But the more they said, the more interested she became. The youth wanted to marry the girl right away, but her father told him he would have to pass a test and prove himself worthy before he could marry his daughter. To prove that he was a good worker, he must plow a field with a team of oxen.

The young man went to the field with the oxen, but instead of working, he sang a song. The words went:

"Amisiminagua he
amisiminagua he
amisiminagua he
amapurma.
    Grotando   grotos,
groto he.
Batata camaná."

As he sang this magic spell, a change came over him,
and he turned into a pig and began plowing the earth
with his nose and eating the snakes and lizards he

turned up in the dirt. The pig was so intent upon plowing that he forgot it was lunchtime and that the girl's brother was to bring him a lunch basket.

The boy arrived with the lunch box and saw the oxen standing idle with no one tending them. Then he noticed a big pig burrowing in the earth. He grew suspicious. Something was not right. The boy hid behind a tree, and it wasn't long before he saw the pig turn back into the youth with gold teeth. He knew then that it was the Devil with whom his sister had fallen in love. Pretending to have seen nothing, he left his hiding place behind the tree and gave the youth the lunch his sister had sent. The youth asked the boy if he had just arrived or if he had seen a pig anywhere. The boy answered no, that he had just arrived and had seen nothing. The youth suspected nothing and pretended to be very tired from the hard morning's work he had done with the oxen.

The boy returned home and told his sister what he had seen, but she would not believe him. He decided to continue spying upon the youth. Every day he watched him go to the field, sing the magic song, and turn into a pig. The boy heard the words so often that he learned them by heart.

At last, since the youth of the gold teeth had passed the test of working the field, the father gave him permission to marry his daughter.

On the wedding day the girl's brother made plans

to disclose the secret to all those who had not believed that the young man was the Devil. The boy hid beneath the table. When all were gathered for the wedding, he began to sing the Devil's song:

"Amisiminagua he
amisiminagua he
amisiminagua he
amapurma.
    Grotando grotos,
groto he.
Batata camaná."

At the sound of the magic words, the young man broke into perspiration. He took off his jacket, then he took off his shirt, and as he was doing this, to the surprise and astonishment of everyone, he began turning into a great black pig. All the wedding guests fled. Only the priest remained with them. The Devil, in the form of a pig, was furious at finding himself caught. He destroyed everything in his way as he tried to reach the girl's brother to kill him. Then the priest took out the crucifix and the holy water and sprinkled some over the pig. The pig ran squealing off into the woods, and the youth with the gold teeth never appeared in that town again.

The girl had learned her lesson, and it wasn't long before she married a young workman of the village.

The Troubadour
and the Devil

(EL VERSADOR Y EL DIABLO)

Long, long ago there were great troubadours who went
from place to place and from city to city singing
the verses they composed. At this time there lived a
young troubadour who was famous for the verses he
could improvise upon any subject. He went from one
village fair to another, singing his songs and accompany-
ing himself with a guitar. He challenged others to
reply to his verses with those of their own. His fame
became so great that no other troubadour dared compete with him.

One day he was invited to go to a fair and take part
in its song contest. When he learned that other popular
troubadours were to be present, he was so sure of himself that he said he didn't care who challenged him,
that he was prepared to compete with the Devil himself.

That night he had been singing constantly—ever
since he had reached the fair—and he had outsung all
the others, who were not clever enough to reply to his
verses. About midnight, just as he thought he had van-
quished them all, a tall, dark man appeared and said

that he had come a long way to compete with the young troubadour whose fame had spread far and wide. The young troubadour saw that his opponent was an expert at making verses and a difficult one to beat. They sang for several hours, and the youth found himself outwitted by his rival's ability to come back with verses that were increasingly difficult to answer. The youth grew suspicious of the man, and his suspicion increased when his opponent sang this verse:

> "I am the fighting cock
> Who carries off the prize.
> And the answer may shock—
> I'm the Devil, baptized."

Upon hearing these words, the youth knew with whom he was competing—it was the Devil himself who had accepted his challenge! The young troubadour decided to fight against the Devil, singing verses he knew the Devil could not answer. He sang:

> "I am the fighting cock
> Of whom you must be wary.
> With words of my Faith I mock
> You—Jesus, Joseph, Mary."

The youth no sooner pronounced these words than the Devil flew off like a tornado, and it is a wonder that the house and all in it were not carried away, too. So the young troubadour was saved, and he never again challenged the Devil.

The Witch's Skin

(LA BRUJA DEL CUERO)

A long time ago, in the days when God walked on earth, a beautiful dancing woman came to a little village. All of the young men fell in love with her, and many died trying to win her. Finally, one of the strongest and bravest of the youths made her his wife and took her home to live in his little cabin.

Every night the wife gave her husband coffee into which she poured a powder to make him sleep soundly until morning. When he was fast asleep, his wife, who was a witch, went out to a guava tree behind their little cabin, and there she took off the skin that covered her witch's body and hung it on the tree. Then she said, "Without God and without Saint Mary," and went flying off through the air to the place where the Devil and the witches danced until dawn. Before the first rays of the sun appeared, the witch flew back to the guava tree, put on her human skin, and lay down beside her husband to wait for him to wake up.

The young man noticed that his wife seemed tired in the morning, as though she had not slept, and that

there was a smell of sulphur about her, which is the odor of the Devil. He suspected that something strange was happening and decided to stay awake and watch.

That night when his wife brought the coffee she had prepared for him, the husband pretended to drink it, but he poured it out in a corner of the cabin. Then he yawned and lay down and pretended to fall asleep. When his wife thought he was truly asleep, she went out to the guava tree. He got up and followed her, hiding behind one of the banana trees, where she could not see him. He saw her take off the human skin that covered her and change into a horrible witch. He was so frightened that he could not move from his hiding place, but he heard his wife say, as she turned into a witch, "Without God and without Saint Mary," and he saw her fly off through the air.

When she had disappeared and the husband had recovered from his fright, he went to the guava tree, took the skin his wife had hung there, and carried it into the kitchen. There he sprinkled it thoroughly with chili, salt, and hot pepper. Then he hung it again on the guava tree just as his wife had left it and went back to his hiding place to wait for the witch to return.

Just before sunrise he saw her come flying to the guava tree. She took down her skin and began putting it on. The chili, salt, and pepper that he had rubbed into the skin began to burn the witch's body. She jumped about and screeched a rasping song:

> "This skin burns, güipindón
> this skin burns, güipindón
> it is not my skin, güipindón
> it is not my skin, güipindón
> Guava! Guava!"

As she sang, she jumped up and down, shouting and clawing at the skin and tearing pieces off.

> "This skin burns, güipindón
> this skin burns, güipindón

> it is not my skin, güipindón
> it is not my skin, güipindón
> Guava! Guava!"

It wasn't long before nothing was left of the skin that covered the horrible witch's body. A ray of sun fell upon her just as the rooster crowed, announcing a new day.

As witches cannot survive being touched by the sun, her body burned up until there was nothing left but ashes. In this way the village was freed from the wicked witch.

The Castle of No Return

(EL CASTILLO DE IRAS Y NO VOLVERAS)

There was once upon a time (and two make three) a man who was so poor that he and his wife had scarcely enough to eat. One day the man went to the river to fish and, after many hours, caught a fish of seven colors. The man was very pleased, thinking that now he and his wife would have food. As he took the hook out and was about to throw the fish into a sack to carry it home, it spoke to him.

"Throw me back into the river, for this is not my day to die. If you come tomorrow, you will be able to catch me and eat me."

The man was so surprised to hear the fish talk that, although he was very hungry, he decided to do as it had told him; and he threw it back into the river. When he returned home, his wife and his dog were waiting at the door to see what he had brought for them to eat. When they found that he had come empty-handed and knew that they would have to go to bed hungry again, the woman began to cry. Her husband consoled her, promising that the next day he would bring her a fine fish.

The next day, very early in the morning, the man left for the river. He fished for many hours without a single bite. As it grew dark and the man was beginning to think that the fish of seven colors had fooled him, he felt a tug on his line, and when he pulled it in, he found that he had caught the fish of seven colors again. As he took the hook out of its mouth, the fish spoke to him.

"Today you may eat me, and because, yesterday, you helped me, I am going to do you a great favor; but you must do exactly as I say. Cut me into three pieces. The head you will give to your horse, the tail to your dog, and you and your wife will eat the body. The scales you must plant behind your house."

The man promised to do as the fish asked and went home, where, before cooking the fish, he divided it as he had been told. That night everyone in the little house slept well and happily after a good meal.

Several months passed, and the man's wife gave birth to three babies, and on the same day the mare had three colts and the dog had three puppies. In the garden where the man had planted the fish scales, there grew three swords. From then on the man and his wife were very happy and had no more troubles in fishing and hunting. The man's sons grew, and each one had his own horse, his own dog, and his own sword. When they became young men, one of them decided to go in search of adventure. His father gave him his blessing, and after saying good-by to his two brothers, the youth set off on his horse, accompanied by his dog. After many days of traveling through the forest, he came to a country where everyone was dressed in mourning and the people in the streets were all crying. The youth was puzzled and asked what had happened to make everyone mourn.

They told him that this was the day when the King had to give one of his daughters to the seven-headed dragon who ruled over the region, threatening to destroy the whole country unless a maiden were given to him each year. The young man asked where the Princess was, and they told him that she was in the distant mountains where the seven-headed dragon lived. The brave youth mounted his horse and rode off to the mountain. Within a few hours he came upon the Princess, who stood crying beneath a tree, for the hour was drawing near when the seven-headed dragon would come for her. The Princess was startled when she saw the youth, and she begged him to flee for his life before the dragon arrived.

The young man told her that he was not afraid of dragons and that he had come to save her from this seven-headed one. The maiden tried to dissuade him, but she saw that he was determined to remain and try to defend her. Just then a snorting was heard as the dragon approached. The maiden began to cry again and begged the youth to go before it was too late. He told her to stay quietly where she was and that he and his dog would take care of the seven-headed dragon.

It wasn't long before the dragon appeared, and even the brave youth, who had never known fear, felt chills run down his spine at the sight of the gigantic monster with seven heads whose mouths opened wide to swallow him and whose noses breathed out smoke and flame. The youth mounted his horse and rode swiftly around the monster, who moved slowly because of his great size. From his saddle he attacked the seven heads, which became distracted in their vain attempts to catch the dog and the horse. So the youth cut away at the dragon's heads with his marvelous sword, and each time a head fell, the monster became angrier but also weaker. Finally, after the battle had lasted several hours, the youth cut off the last head and the dragon fell down dead. The Princess, who had watched it all, could not contain her joy at being saved from the fearful monster. She threw her arms about the brave youth and kissed him. He gathered up the seven heads and tied them to his horse's tail. Then he lifted the Princess up on the saddle beside him and rode off to the castle to return the King's daughter.

People in the castle had heard the dragon scream each time a head was cut off, but they did not know what had happened in the mountain. Only when they saw the youth coming with the Princess and the seven dragon heads did they understand, and there was great rejoicing. For seven days and seven nights, the people danced to celebrate the end of the monster who had laid waste their country and caused them so much suffering. The King, to show his gratitude to the youth, gave him his daughter in marriage; and there was a splendid wedding. The youth lived in the castle with the Princess, and he was very happy there.

One day he and the Princess climbed the highest tower in the castle to look out across the countryside. As they were admiring the view from the high tower, they noticed a castle in the distance that seemed very grand and beautiful. The youth asked the Princess whose it was, and she told him that it was the "Castle of No Return," an enchanted castle from which none who entered ever came back. The youth, who knew no fear, told the Princess that he was going to the castle the very next day. The Princess was so happy with her husband that she tried to make him change his mind. If he went, she said, he would never return, and she loved him so much that she could not bear to lose him. The youth, who craved adventure, quieted her fears, telling her not to worry, that he would return.

The next day, as the sun rose, he mounted his horse and rode off, accompanied by his dog. After many hours of riding, he reached the Castle of No Return just as the sun was setting and found nothing unusual about it. When he entered the great hall, he met a little old woman who sat there spinning. She greeted him and asked him to tie his horse and his dog outside as they frightened her. The youth, who liked the little old woman, told her that he had no rope with which to tie them. She pulled some long hairs from her head and gave them to him. With these he tied the horse and the dog. When the old woman saw that the animals were tied fast, she challenged him to wrestle with her. Believing the old woman to be weak, he accepted the challenge, and they began to wrestle in the great hall of the castle. It wasn't long before the youth became aware that he was wrestling with a witch who had great magic strength, and he called to his animals for help. But the witch's hair had turned into chains, so that the horse could not bring him the sword that hung from its saddle, nor could the dog come to his aid. It was not long before the old woman overcame him, and he lost consciousness. She dragged him to the edge of a well and sprinkled him, his horse, and his dog with the magic water. It turned them all into stones similar to the ones already lying there.

Now, back home, the youth's two brothers were very worried by his long absence. One day, as one of the brothers was cleaning his sword, he saw drops of blood upon it. He knew immediately that some misfortune had befallen his absent brother, and he went to his father and asked permission to go in search of him.

The father agreed and gave him his blessing. So the second brother set out with his horse and his dog in search of the lost one.

After traveling a long way, he reached the country where his brother had killed the dragon, and because the three boys were identical in appearance, everyone mistook him for his brother and thought that he was the Princess's husband who had come back from the Castle of No Return. He allowed them to believe this in order to find out what had happened to his brother. The Princess also mistook him for her husband and was very happy that he had at last returned from the enchanted castle. The youth said nothing, but he knew now where he had to search for his brother.

Early the next morning he left for the Castle of No Return. When he reached it, he found the old witch, and the same things happened again—she made him tie up his horse and his dog, and she overcame him and turned him to stone.

Back at home, the third brother knew that a misfortune had befallen the second one as well, for now it was his sword on which the blood appeared. He asked permission to go in search of his brothers, and the father, saddened at the thought of losing all his sons, gave him his blessing.

The young man rode for many days until he came to the same country his brothers had reached. The King, the Princess, and all the people thought he was the man who had killed the dragon and that he had returned for the second time from the Castle of No Return. The Princess was so happy to have him back that she begged him never to go to the enchanted castle again. The youth said nothing but listened to everything in order to find out what had happened to his two brothers.

That very night, when everyone was fast asleep, he mounted his horse and rode off with his dog to the Castle of No Return. It was still night when he reached it, and he hid to watch and see what went on in the castle. He saw the old woman dancing and jumping about as only witches do at night; so he knew what she was. In the morning, he watched her dress as an old woman and sit down to spin in the great hall. He went in, and the old woman told him, just as she had told his brothers, to tie his horse and his dog outside as she was afraid of them. When he said he had no rope, she pulled out two long hairs and gave them to him. But knowing she was a witch, the youth only pretended to tie the animals. When she thought that the horse and the dog were chained, she invited the youth to wrestle with her, and he accepted. During the struggle, he saw that her strength was far greater than his. He called to his animals, saying, "Come, my horse, bring my sword! Come, my faithful dog!"

When they heard their master's voice, the horse and the dog ran to him. He managed to free himself from the witch and jump into the saddle, where he grasped his sword and began slashing at her with it. At the same time, his dog attacked her. In her great anger at seeing herself outnumbered, the old witch fought even more ferociously. But it was no use—the youth beheaded her.

As he reached for the head, it spoke to him, saying that since he had won, he must burn the body and make an ointment of the ashes. This he must rub on the stones that were lying about and so break the evil spell that lay upon the castle. The youth did this, and, to his amazement, there appeared princes, kings, warriors, and princesses who had been turned into stones by the witch. Among them were his two brothers. They greeted each other joyfully. Then, with all the others whom the youth had saved, they went back to the King's castle. The Princess could not tell which of the three brothers was her husband. They explained everything, and the first son made himself known as her husband. The King asked the other two brothers to marry his two remaining daughters. This they were happy to do. Later, they sent for their parents, and all lived happily for many years.

The evil spell that had been cast over the Castle of No Return was broken forever.

Juanito and the Princess
(JUANITO Y LA PRINCESA)

Once upon a time there was a boy named Juanito. His
mother was dead, and he lived with his poor old father
who worked very hard so that his son need never go
hungry.

Juanito wanted to travel, have adventures, and earn
money to help his father. So one day he announced
that he was leaving. The father was not happy to have
his son go, but he knew how the boy felt, so he gave
his permission. As Juanito was leaving the house, his
father asked which he would rather have, money or
his blessing.

Juanito said, "Father, give me your blessing, but keep
the money for the things you may need." His father
blessed him, and Juanito left.

After many days of walking through the forest, he
met a lion, an eagle, and an ant who were quarreling
over a dead ox. Juanito tried to keep from being seen,
but they spied him and called him to them. He thought
surely the lion would eat him up, but when he came
up to the animals, they told him not to be afraid, that
they only wanted him to do them the favor of dividing

the dead ox among them. They themselves had not been able to agree as to which part of the animal should go to which one of them. Juanito, who was glad that the animals were not thinking of harming him, said, "If you accept my way of dividing the ox, I agree to help you." The animals said yes, that they would respect his decision. Then Juanito told the lion that his part was the flesh, that the ant was to have the bones, and that the entrails were to go to the eagle. The animals were satisfied with this division, and each one began to take his share. Juanito said good-by to them and left. But he hadn't gone far when he heard them call. He returned, and they explained that, since he had done them a good turn, each one wished to give him something.

The lion spoke up first and said, "Pull a hair from my tail, and any time you may need me say, 'God and the Lion,' and you will turn into a lion as strong as I."

Then the eagle spoke and said, "Pull a feather from my head, and any time you may need me say, 'God and the Eagle,' and you will turn into an eagle as powerful as I."

Finally the ant spoke and said, "Juanito, pull off one of my legs, and any time you may need me say, 'God and the Ant,' and you will turn into an ant as tiny as I."

Juanito followed their instructions and put the lion's hair, the eagle's feather, and the ant's leg in his pocket and set off on his way through the forest.

After walking for seven days and seven nights, he came to a mountain where there was a great castle with a very high tower. Juanito tried to enter the castle, but there was no door. Then he noticed a window at the top of the tower and decided to test the gift the eagle had given him. Taking out the feather, he said, "God and the Eagle," and found himself turned into an eagle. He spread his wings and flew up to the tower window. As he alighted, he saw a beautiful young girl who became frightened at the sight of the eagle. Juanito spoke to her and told her not to be afraid, that he was a young man who had turned into an eagle in order to reach her window. Then, to quiet her fears, he said, "God and Man," and changed himself into a man. The Princess was delighted to be able to talk with another human being and told Juanito that she was a princess who had been taken by a giant in her childhood and held captive in the tower ever since.

Brave Juanito fell in love with the Princess and promised her that he would fight and kill the giant and set her free. The maiden told him that many had tried to do this, but that the giant had killed them all. No one could kill the giant because his life lay outside his body, where swords and arrows could do it no harm. Then the Princess, who had fallen in love with Juanito, begged him to flee before the giant came. Juanito told her that he was going to find out where the giant kept his life; then he would search out that place and take it and kill the giant. As they were talking, they heard a noise and knew the giant was coming. Juanito took out the ant's leg and said, "God and the Ant," turned himself into an ant, and hid in a crack in the floor.

The giant arrived and asked the Princess with whom she was talking. The Princess replied that she was talking with no one—as he could see, there was no one in the room. The giant searched, and as he found no one, he asked the Princess if she talked to herself, for he *had* heard her talking. She told him that she had been dreaming that he had eaten a poisoned deer and had died. The giant burst out laughing and said that he could eat all the poison in the world and not die since his life was safely hidden somewhere else. He was drinking wine, and each time he emptied his huge cup, the Princess filled it again to keep him talking in hopes that he might reveal his secret.

After a while, the giant became intoxicated and told her that his life lay in the head of a porcupine; that in the porcupine's head there was a dove, and in the dove there was an egg, and that breaking this egg was the only way of killing him. The giant told her all this because he was sure that no one would be able to do it; but Juanito was listening to everything from his crack in the floor and had made up his mind what to do.

That night, while the giant slept, Juanito said, "God and Man," and became a man again. He assured the Princess that that very day he would go in search of the porcupine that held the giant's life. After kissing the Princess good-by, he said, "God and the Eagle," and flew off in search of the porcupine.

After many days, news reached him of a man whose

sheep were being killed by a porcupine. Juanito went to see the man and asked for a job looking after his sheep. The man replied that no one wanted that work since a porcupine attacked the shepherd and ate the sheep. Juanito said he would take the job nonetheless and went off up the mountain to tend the sheep. He took out the lion's hair and said, "God and the Lion," turned himself into a lion, and pounced upon the porcupine. They fought furiously all that day until both were exhausted and the porcupine begged for a truce, saying, "If I were in my mud hole, I could beat this man!"

And Juanito answered, "If I had a cup of wine, a piece of bread, and a maiden's kiss, I could kill you!"

Then each one retired, agreeing to continue the fight the next day. Now the daughter of the man who had engaged Juanito as his shepherd was hiding there and saw everything that happened. She ran to tell her father. He told her to take wine and bread to Juanito the next day and to give him a kiss, and they would see if he could kill the porcupine.

The next day the porcupine returned, and Juanito, in the form of a lion, attacked him. They fought all morning and all afternoon. Then the porcupine said, "If I were in my mud hole, I could beat this man!"

Juanito replied, "If I had a cup of wine, a piece of bread, and a maiden's kiss, I could kill you!"

No sooner had he said this than the owner's daughter appeared and gave him a cup of wine, which Juanito swallowed at one gulp, a piece of bread, which he ate at one bite, and a kiss. Juanito pounced upon the porcupine and killed it. Then he said, "God and Man," turned himself into a man, and cut open the porcupine's head. Before he could catch it, a black dove flew out of the head and away. Juanito took out the eagle's feather and said, "God and the Eagle," and flew after the dove. He caught it in his claws and dragged it to the ground; then, turning himself back into a man, he opened the dove and took a black egg out of its heart. This was where the giant's life lay. Juanito turned himself into an eagle and flew off with it to the Princess's tower.

When she saw him coming, she was very happy; and when he told her all that had happened and that he had the egg which held the giant's life, she gave him a kiss.

Just then the giant came and was greatly astonished to see Juanito, for he could not understand how he had been able to get in. The giant was furious and tried to catch Juanito to kill him; but as he was so big, he moved slowly, and Juanito kept him running up and down the tower until he was tired out. Then Juanito let him come close and threw the egg at his head. The moment the egg broke, the giant fell to the ground, dead.

At the giant's death, the Princess was free. She and Juanito married, took possession of all the giant's riches, and lived happily for many years, and Juanito's old father came to live with them.

The Singing Sack

(EL ZURRON QUE CANTABA)

There was once a very beautiful girl named White
Flower. It was her habit to go to the river to bathe with
her brothers. One day, while taking her bath, she re-
moved the golden earrings her mother had given her
and laid them on a stone for safekeeping. It was growing
dark when the children finished bathing, and they made
haste to hurry home. On the way, White Flower remembered that she had left her earrings on the stone,
and although it was now night and quite dark, she left
her brothers and returned to the river to get them.
They were not there!

As she searched, suddenly she heard a voice say, "My
child, is this what you are looking for?" and there stood
an old man with her earrings in his hand. In her delight
at finding them, White Flower did not notice what an
unpleasant old man he was, and she ran to him to take
her earrings. He grabbed her and thrust her into a sack
he was carrying. When he had tied the sack securely,
he told White Flower that she must stay there and that
she must sing whenever he commanded her to, and if

she didn't, he would stick her with a spike. Then the
old man threw the sack across his shoulder and set off
for the village.

White Flower's mother waited all night for her to
return, and when she did not come, her mother knew
that something very bad had happened to her. Days
passed with no news of White Flower until everyone believed that she had fallen into the river and drowned.

Meanwhile, the old man went from house to house
with the sack, collecting money from the village people
to hear it sing. At each house he would say:

> "Sack, sing! Sing, sack!
> Sharp spike pricks back!"

And White Flower would sing:

> "Your golden earrings, Mother,
> I tried to keep dry.
> So in this sack I smother,
> For earrings I must die."

People were enthralled by the sweet voice that issued
from the sack, and they gave money to the old man.
So he continued going from house to house, until, without knowing it, he came to the house of White Flower's
mother.

> "Sack, sing! Sing, sack!
> Sharp spike pricks back!"

And White Flower sang her sad song:

> "Your golden earrings, Mother,
> I tried to keep dry.
> So in this sack I smother,
> For earrings I must die."

When White Flower's mother heard the song, she recognized her daughter's voice, and immediately she understood what had happened to her dear child. Pretending to suspect nothing, she invited the old man to come in and have something to eat, but to leave his sack outside. The old man, who was too greedy to spend money for food, accepted. He left his sack outside by the door and followed the mother into the kitchen. While he was eating, White Flower's brothers opened the sack and rescued their sister. Then they filled the sack with mud and cow dung.

When the old man finished his meal, he came out, picked up the sack, and prepared to set off to earn more money with it. White Flower's mother told him that he ought to make his sack sing for the King, who would give him a good sum of money.

So the old man went to the palace and asked the King if he would like to hear the magic sack. The King said yes, to please make it sing.

So the old man, thinking the girl was still inside, said:

"Sack, sing! Sing, sack!
Sharp spike pricks back!"

No song came from the sack. The King grew impatient, and the old man grew desperate.

"Sack, sing! Sing, sack!
Sharp spike pricks back!"

Still no song came. The old man's anger rose at the thought that the girl dared to disobey him. He grew very angry and thrust the sharp spike through the sack. The sack tore open, and mud and cow dung fell out and splashed all over the King and the court.

The King, thinking the old man had done it purposely to play a trick on him, called the soldiers and had the old man thrown into a dungeon for the rest of his days. And so he paid for what he had done to White Flower.

Lazy Peter and the King

(PEDRO ANIMALA Y EL REY)

There was once a man called Lazy Peter. He was something of a rascal who spent his time thinking up mischief. The King had threatened to have him beheaded the next time he was caught at one of his pranks.

It wasn't long before Peter was caught deceiving some priests and was brought before the King. The King, by this time tired of Peter's mischief, condemned him to death. He ordered that Peter be put in a sack and thrown off a cliff into the sea.

The soldiers seized Peter, put him in a sack, tied it tightly, and carried it to the cliff. Before throwing it over, they told Peter he could make one request. Peter answered from the sack, begging them not to throw him over until they brought a priest who could hear his confession and absolve him of his sins.

Since they could not kill a man without giving him the opportunity of commending his soul to God, the soldiers agreed and told Peter they would leave him there and come back the next day with a priest.

A few hours after they had gone, Peter heard the

bleating of sheep and goats and knew that a shepherd and his herd were passing by. He began to cry out in a loud voice, "No! No! No, I won't marry her!" One of the shepherds walked over to the sack and asked what was the matter and why was he shouting, "I won't marry her."

Peter answered that the King had tied him in the sack because he wouldn't marry the Princess. The shepherd replied that he would rather marry a Princess than be a shepherd. This was just what Peter wanted to hear. He offered to change places with the shepherd.

"If you let me out, I'll tie you in the sack, and then you can marry the Princess," he said.

The shepherd opened the sack and let Peter out; then he crawled in. After Peter had tied the sack securely, he rounded up the herd of sheep and goats and hid nearby to watch what happened.

The next morning the soldiers arrived with the priest.

"The priest is here," they said when they came to the sack. "Now say what you have to say."

The shepherd, who thought the priest had come to marry him to the King's daughter, shouted like an idiot, "Yes! Yes! I want to marry the Princess!"

Hearing this, the priest and the soldiers thought surely Peter had lost his mind. The priest hurriedly blessed the sack and left. The soldiers picked it up and tossed it over the cliff into the sea.

A few days later, Peter appeared in the town with

his herd of sheep and goats. Since everyone had thought him dead, there was much consternation at seeing him alive. It caused a great commotion. The soldiers arrested him again and brought him before the King. He was more dismayed than anyone and asked Peter where he had come from. Smiling, Peter answered that he had come from the bottom of the sea to thank the King for throwing him in, because it was there, at the bottom, he had found riches and the herd of sheep and goats.

The King, who was very greedy, ordered that he himself be thrown into the sea at the exact spot from which they had thrown Peter.

Everyone is still waiting for him to return.

Juan Bobo and the
Princess Who Answered Riddles

(JUAN BOBO Y LA PRINCESA
ADIVINADORA)

Once upon a time there was a king who was very fond of riddles. He had a talented daughter who was clever at solving them, no matter how difficult they might be.

The King wanted his daughter to marry a man who was as intelligent as she was, so he decided that she should marry the first man who could ask her a riddle that she could not solve. He posted a proclamation to this effect all over the kingdom, but he also made it clear that any man who failed in the test should have his head cut off.

As the Princess was very beautiful, ever so many princes and noblemen were eager to marry her, so there were great numbers of applicants. But, alas! The beautiful Princess was able to solve all of their riddles. It wasn't long before the castle walls were covered with the heads of those who had failed to win the Princess.

In this country there lived a poor widow who had an only son named Juan. Because he was a rather foolish fellow who didn't seem to know his right hand from his left, people called him Juan Bobo, which means

Simple John. One day as Juan Bobo was walking by
the castle walls, he looked at the heads of the princes
and noblemen who had failed to win the Princess by
their cleverness. It occurred to him that he might be
able to succeed where they had failed. That day Juan
Bobo came home earlier than usual and told his mother
that he was going to try his luck at the castle and see
if he could win the Princess. His mother cried and
begged him not to think of it, reminding him of the
numbers who had tried and failed and lost their heads,
princes and noblemen and all much more intelligent
than Juan Bobo; so, how could he think of doing such
a foolish thing! But neither her arguments nor her
tears were of any avail. Juan Bobo insisted that the next
morning early he would leave on his donkey for the
King's castle, and he knew he would be able to catch
the beautiful Princess with a riddle.

When his mother saw that it was useless to try to dissuade him, she stopped trying and prepared two cakes
for Juan to take with him—all the food she had in the
house. She was so upset and her eyes were so filled with
tears that she could not see clearly, and she seasoned
them with a poisonous powder instead of sprinkling
salt upon them.

Early the next morning, after saying good-by to his
mother, who was still crying that she would never see
her son again, Juan Bobo mounted his old donkey,
named Panda, and set out for the castle. After several

hours of travel, he dismounted and stretched out on the grass at the edge of the road to rest and to think up a riddle that the Princess would not be able to solve. While Juan Bobo lay there dreaming, the donkey broke open the lunch basket and ate the poisoned cakes. In no time at all she rolled over and died. Three vultures, flying overhead, swooped down and made a meal of the dead donkey, and since she had been poisoned, they, too, died.

When Juan Bobo awoke and saw them lying there —the dead donkey and the three dead vultures—he knew immediately what had happened because the cakes were gone. Since he was hungry, he took his gun to hunt for food. He spied a wild rabbit and shot at it, but missed and killed another rabbit, which at that moment jumped in the path of his bullet. Juan Bobo cooked and ate it and found he was thirsty. As he had no water, he climbed a coconut tree, cut off one of the nuts, and drank the juice. He had to go the rest of the way to the castle on foot. As he walked along, his mind was filled with thoughts of his donkey, Panda, the vultures, the rabbit, and the coconut. Since he had as yet thought of no riddle, he decided to make one up out of the adventures that had befallen him that morning.

When Juan Bobo reached the castle and told the guards what he had come for, they laughed and laughed. They knew him and how stupid he was, and they were not going to let him in. But Juan Bobo insisted that the proclamation applied to everyone, and he was within his rights in accepting the King's invitation. So the guards finally went to the King and told him that Juan Bobo was outside with a riddle for the Princess. At first the King was indignant that a country bumpkin should dare think himself worthy of marrying his daughter. Then he remembered his promise that she should marry the man, rich or poor, nobleman or commoner, whose riddle she could not solve, and he ordered the guards to bring Juan Bobo in.

Juan Bobo walked into the throne room, past the King and his court, over to where the Princess was waiting for him. He greeted her and said:

> "I left home with Panda,
> And two killed her;
> But Panda killed three.
> I shot at what I saw,
> But killed what I didn't see.
> I was thirsty and drank
> Water which never sank
> Into earth nor fell from sky.
> If you guess my conundrum,
> Princess, I'm done-drum!"

The Princess thought and thought and thought, and, to the great surprise of the King and the court, she could not find the answer. Now, according to the rules the King had made, she was allowed three days in which to find the solution. So Juan Bobo was lodged in the castle for three days while she was thinking.

The first night the Princess sent one of her hand-maidens to Juan's room to see if she could get the answer from him. The girl was very beautiful, but Juan Bobo paid no attention to her chatter.

The second night the Princess sent her lady-in-waiting, who was even more beautiful. But her efforts, too, were futile. Juan would say nothing.

The third night the Princess, in desperation, went herself and begged him to tell her the solution to his riddle. After she had begged a long time, Juan Bobo agreed to tell her the answer if she, in turn, would give him her ring and one of her shoes. The Princess did not hesitate—she gave him her ring and a shoe. Then Juan Bobo explained how he had left home on his donkey, Panda; how she had died after eating the poisoned cakes; how the three vultures had also been poisoned when they ate Panda; how he had fired at a rabbit, missed it, and killed another; and how he had quenched his thirst with coconut water.

As soon as the Princess heard this, she clapped her hands and ran from the room.

The next day the court assembled in the throne room to hear the Princess solve Juan Bobo's riddle. She had no trouble at all. Before them all, she gave the explanation Juan had given her the night before.

The King was very happy when he saw that he would not have to be the father-in-law of an ignorant country bumpkin. He called the headsman and ordered him to cut off Juan Bobo's head and put it on the wall with the others.

As the headsman started to carry out the order, Juan Bobo asked permission to speak, and the King granted his request. Then Juan told how the Princess had obtained the answer from him and how she had come to his room begging for it the night before. As proof, he showed the ring and the shoe that the Princess had given him.

The King was a just man. He ordered that the sentence of execution be suspended and that a wedding be celebrated instead of a beheading.

Thus it was that the fool of the town married the Princess and, after a while, became the King of the country.

Count Crow and
the Princess

(EL CONDE CUERVO Y LA PRINCESA)

In the Kingdom of Long Ago there was a king who had
a very beautiful but vain and silly daughter. The Princess was old enough to marry but, until now, had refused all the princes, counts, and dukes who had fallen
in love with her. She found fault with them all, making
fun of them and giving them ridiculous nicknames.

One day the King, very concerned about his daughter's conduct and wanting her to marry so there would
be an heir to the throne, called all the eligible young
men in the kingdom to the palace so that the Princess
might choose one of them for her husband. From all
parts came princes, dukes, counts, and noblemen. All
of them wanted to marry the Princess. The King gave
a big party, and one by one the guests came forward
to meet her. As each one came before her, she laughed
at him and made fun of him. If the young man was
thin, she called him Duke Bones; if he was stout, she
called him Count Big-Belly; if he was short, she called
him Prince Dwarf. She laughed and embarrassed them
all before the whole court.

Among the noblemen who had come to the party, there was a count who had a long nose. He was very much in love with the Princess, but as he bent to kiss her hand, the Princess burst out laughing and said that he must be Count Crow, for he certainly looked like one. The Count was humiliated and decided to settle matters with the Princess.

Meantime, the King was furious, for his daughter's haughty behavior reflected upon him, so that he was in bad standing with all the noblemen whom she had refused. So angry was he that he told his daughter that, since she had turned down all the noblemen whom he had invited to the palace, he was going to force her to marry the first beggar who came asking for alms.

When the King said this, the Count whom the Princess had called Count Crow was listening, and he decided that this was his chance. The next day Count Crow came to the palace dressed in the ragged clothes of a beggar and asked the King for alms. The King then called the Princess and, reminding her of his threat, told her that she had to marry the beggar. The Princess burst into tears, crying no, that she would never marry a dirty beggar! But her father said that she had to, for he had given the word of a king. Right then and there he called a priest, who married the Princess to the beggar.

Count Crow told the Princess that now she had to come and live with him in his hut, and he led her off, stumbling along the road. It was a long way they had to go, and the Princess was not used to walking. She grew very tired, and her feet were cut by the sharp stones. As they passed a handsome palace, the Princess asked her husband if they could stop there to rest. But the Count told her that beggars were not allowed there, so they had to go on. The Princess asked whose palace it was, and he told her that it belonged to a nobleman called Count Crow. The Princess felt very sad to remember that she had refused him. They went on a little farther until they came to a fountain. The Princess wanted to stop for a drink of the fresh water, but her husband said they couldn't because the fountain belonged to Count Crow, and one had to have his permission to drink its water. The Princess was so thirsty! She suffered terribly, thinking how different things would have been had she accepted the Count's offer of marriage. At last they reached a cabin, and the Count or beggar, whichever you will, said to his wife, "This is our home." It had only one room and no furniture at all. When the Princess saw it and compared it with the richness of Count Crow's palace, she began to cry, for she realized that all had happened this way because of her vanity and arrogance.

In his heart, the Count felt sorry for her, but he still wanted to be sure she had learned her lesson, so he said nothing. The next morning he told her to go to the forest and fetch wood for the fire so that he could have breakfast. The Princess, who had never cooked, didn't know what to do. She began to cry, but the Count told her to stop crying and get to work. So she went up the mountainside with an ax and after a while brought back a few scraps of dirty, wet kindling. When she tried to light it, she burned her fingers, and after she got the fire going, she didn't know how to cook. The Count helped her by explaining. Though she followed his directions as best she could through her tears, everything turned out badly, and she kept burning her fingers on the pots.

In the afternoon the Count came home laden with a great pile of earthen pots, vases, casseroles, and bowls and told his wife to take them to the marketplace and sell them, for she must help him earn a living.

The Princess did not know how she was to carry all these things, but the Count balanced the whole cargo on her head and sent her off to the market. There she arranged her pots and jars about her on the ground and began to call out her wares to the passersby. The Count ordered the cavalry to gallop through the street so that their horses' hoofs broke all the pottery. The Princess came home in tears to wait for her husband. He arrived before long and looked surprised to find her there. "Home so early? Did you sell all your merchandise?" Through her sobs the Princess explained how the soldiers had broken everything. The Count said that was too bad, but as they had nothing to eat, she must find something.

The Princess answered that she did not know where to get food, and her husband said, "Tonight there is to be a great wedding party at Count Crow's palace, for he is being married. You go to the palace and find work in the kitchen. Bring home to me the leftovers they'll give you there."

The Princess thought again how different things could have been for her if she had accepted Count Crow's offer; but she had begun to be truly fond of her husband, so she went to the palace. They gave her work in the kitchen, where she carefully gathered leftover scraps of food and put them into a bag that she fastened to a belt beneath her skirts.

Meantime, the Count had taken off his beggar's rags and stood receiving his guests, handsomely dressed in his best clothes.

When all were seated at the table, the Count told the cook to have the girl who was working in the kitchen bring in one of the great, heavy platters. When the cook gave the Princess this order, she trembled with fear. She was afraid Count Crow might recognize her. When she came into the dining hall with the great, heavy platter of food, the bag of leftovers she had hidden beneath her skirts fell out on the floor. All the guests laughed, and the Princess's eyes were filled with tears of shame as she ran back into the kitchen. Seeing her humiliation, Count Crow rose from the table and followed her.

"Dry your tears and look at me," he said. "Do you know who I am?"

She did not dare to look but answered through her sobs, "Yes. You are the Count."

Then he lifted her head and made her look at him, and when she saw how much he resembled her beggar husband, suddenly she understood. The Count then explained what he had done and asked her forgiveness for having made her suffer so much. He told her that he had wanted to teach her a lesson so that she would give up her vain and foolish ways.

Since the Princess had fallen in love with the Count, she forgave him and they went back to the banquet hall together. Count Crow then presented her to all as his wife. And after that they lived happily in the palace, for the Princess had learned to live like the rest of the people in her kingdom.